Caper Steals Christmas

A Tiny House Mystery, Book Six

By Cynthia Hickey

DEDICATION

To all those who love a good surprise at Christmas.

Chapter One

I hung an ornament on the Christmas tree in the newly erected community hall. Now, we could have gatherings all year round, and our Christmas party would be the first big event.

The building took up the space where half the playground had been dug up after some serious issues with the local drug dealers a few months ago. Rather than repair the playground, we simply moved it over and built the community hall. Since the owner was my uncle, I could pretty much do anything I wanted with the place.

"CJ Turley," A voice scolded from behind me. I turned and smiled at my friend, Mags Snyder. "You know the tree should have some kind of a theme. This looks like a child decorated it. You've every color of the rainbow and then some."

I frowned, scrunching my nose. "These are my grandmother's ornaments. I like the ornaments to be a little of everything. You'll remember I did offer to let you take care of the décor, and you declined." I hung an obscenely large bulb at eye level just for spite.

Mags groaned. "I hope somebody steals that thing."

I whirled back to face her. "Take that back. Some of these are antiques." Maybe I shouldn't have used Grams's things, but I couldn't put a tree in my tiny house big enough for more than three or five bulbs. I wanted to share my treasures with those around me.

"Well, I think it's gaudy."

"It's gorgeous." Eric Drake, local park ranger and my boyfriend, entered the building as Mags continued her criticism. "But not as lovely as my girl." He lowered his head and kissed me.

"Hello to you, too." I smiled.

"Do you know where your dog is?" He stepped back. "Because she's causing trouble, chasing the new tenant's cat, or so they've complained."

I groaned. Caper only wanted to play, but not all four-legged, or two-legged, creatures for that matter, reciprocated my feisty pup's feelings. "Can you catch her and lock her in the house?"

"Already done. Just wanted you to know that house number fifteen isn't happy."

"Thanks. I'll stop by there when I'm finished here." I stepped back and surveyed the tree again. It was perfect. Grabbing my jacket, I headed for the door. "See y'all later."

A brisk wind blew off the mountain rising above Heavenly Acres. The winter sun sparkled off Blue Lake. I really loved where I lived, despite the recent crimes that had begun over the year I'd worked here as manager. Things had settled down for the time being, and life was good.

I climbed into my red and white golf cart and drove around the loop to house number fifteen. Hoping the couple who lived there, Lee and Kim Westford, were reasonable people, I hopped from the cart and knocked on their front door.

A fluffy white cat blinked at me from the windowsill. The pretty thing didn't look any the worse after Caper's romp with her, which eased my nerves.

Mrs. Westford, a slightly plump, well-dressed woman in her mid-fifties, answered the door. "What are you going to do about that dog?"

Okay, not reasonable. "I apologize. Caper is not normally away from me. Is your cat alright?"

"No thanks to that mutt, Sugar is just fine. I had to give her extra salmon to make up for the stress of the chase. When we rented this house, you assured us we could reside here in peace."

Caper was not a mutt. Well, I didn't know if she was purebred or not, but in my heart she was a show dog. "I'll do my best to fulfill that promise, Mrs. Westford." I glanced over to where the bored-looking feline licked its paw. "Sugar is very pretty."

"She ought to be. She's a Norwegian Forest Cat with a long bloodline and cost us a thousand dollars. She's won awards." The woman actually lifted her chin and sniffed like an aristocrat.

Wow. I couldn't imagine spending that much money on an animal. "She, uh, looks worth every penny." No wonder they had to live in a tiny house.

They probably spent all their money on the cat.

I shoved aside the uncharitable thought and turned to leave. Before I was off the porch, Sugar darted between my legs. I windmilled my arms and fell, bouncing down the steps. I'd call Caper and the cat even.

"Sugar," Mrs. Westford darted past me after the white ball of fur streaking down the road.

"I'm okay. I can get up by myself." I rolled my eyes and groaned. Nothing felt broken, thank God.

By the time I limped to my cart, Mags was speeding my way on her cart. "That cat is in your Christmas tree."

Oh, no. My ornaments! Sugar was starting to be a real pain in my behind, and that had nothing to do with my tumble down the stairs.

Shoving aside my aches and pains, I sped back to the community center. Thank goodness the tree still stood, but a white paw flicked out from inside the tree and batted at the large bulb I'd hung last.

"Mrs. Westford, please remove your cat from the tree." I put my hands on my hips and glared at the woman who sat, smiling, in a padded chair.

"She loves Christmas trees."

"These are my personal belongings that belonged to my grandmother. I'd really appreciate your cat not breaking them."

"Very well." She unfolded herself from the chair and carefully retrieved Sugar. "Have you considered a higher fence at the entrance here? I'm afraid Sugar can climb over or under the one we have."

"Mrs. Westford, I cannot put in a new gate for

a cat." I fought the urge to roll my eyes again.

"This is going to be a long six-month lease." Back straight, she marched from the building.

I agreed with her. Six months would seem like an eternity if there were more days like today.

Less than two minutes later, Mrs. Westford returned. "Where is her collar?"

"Excuse me?"

"Sugar's collar is missing." She shoved the cat into my arms and made a dash for the tree. "I don't see it." Her frantic searching knocked several ornaments from the tree. One shattered, and the large bulb rolled across the floor and lodged under the tree.

"Be careful, please." I tightened my grip on the squirming animal and received a scratch for my trouble. "Could she have lost it on the way here? Do you have another one?"

She narrowed her eyes. "That one is crusted with diamonds!"

"Why in the world would you have a diamond collar on a pet?" A jewel thief had once switched the rhinestones on Caper's collar to diamonds, but that was to hide the jewels in plain sight, not because my dog was spoiled.

"We bought it as a reward when she won her first ribbon." She took the cat from me. "She earned it."

"Let's fetch my dog and retrace her steps. Caper has a talent for finding jewels." Unfortunately for me in the past. I eyed Sugar. "Maybe we'll take her home first."

I drove Mrs. Westford to her house to drop off the cat, then she rode with me to retrieve Caper.

My little spaniel wasn't a genius or anything, but she definitely seemed to understand me when I talked to her. "Please hold out your wedding ring to her so she'll know we're looking for diamonds."

"Are you serious?" Mrs. Westford's eyes widened.

"Yes, ma'am."

Scowling, she held out her hand for Caper to sniff, recoiling as my pup's nose touched her skin. "I detest dogs."

"Be nice or she won't help." I knelt. "Find the diamonds, girl."

Caper barked once, wagged her tail, and took off with her nose to the ground. Diamonds, cats, and squirrels were what got my dog excited.

"What's going on?" Mags stopped next to us.

"An expensive collar fell off the cat's neck," I said.

"She has a name, you know. Her name is Sugar." Mrs. Westford clamped her lips together.

"You sent Caper to find it?" Mags grinned. "That'll work. Hop in."

Mrs. Westford took the seat next to Mags, leaving me to hang onto the back. It wasn't the first time. Most of the time I actually enjoyed it, but my body was violently protesting my thumps down the stairs. I started to think I might have bruised my tailbone.

Caper slowed and glanced back at us, then continued forward again. She ran a circle around house number fifteen, then darted for the park, empty of children on the cold day. She squeezed under a bush and barked.

Bingo. I hopped off the cart and rushed toward her. "Okay, let me see." I pulled her out.

In her mouth was a collar with half the diamonds missing. "Looks like someone got scared and tossed this." I glanced around the area.

With no rain in a few days, there weren't any footprints. I didn't need anyone to know we had a diamond thief among us. Again.

Who and how did they know the diamonds on the cat's collar were real? And how did they manage to remove so many in such a short amount of time?

Chapter Two

Mrs. Westford yanked the collar from my hand. "I cannot believe this is happening."

Neither could I, to be honest. Theft and murder were getting old. At least it was just a collar. Hopefully, the woman had taken out insurance on something so valuable. Animals tended to get their collars hung on things when running around outside. "Time to call Davis."

Mags' grandson-in-law was our local detective. He wouldn't be happy, or surprised, about another mystery at Heavenly Acres.

Mr. Westford arrived at the community hall at the same time as Davis. While he had a worried look on his face, the detective looked more resigned than upset.

I went through the spiel of what had happened up to finding Sugar in the Christmas tree. Before I could finish, Davis had moved on.

Sighing, he parted the branches on the Christmas tree, lowered himself to his knees, and looked up, then circled it twice. "I don't see anything."

"It's here." Mrs. Westford held up the collar.

Davis blinked a few times. "I thought it was missing."

"It was." She shook her head. "We found it with half the diamonds missing."

"If you hadn't been in such a hurry to be through with this," I said, "you'd know that I didn't have time to tell you the whole story." Seriously, was I that bad to be around that he couldn't stay long enough to hear all the facts?

"Sorry." Davis crossed his arms. "Mrs. Westford, kindly finish." When she did, he asked, "Do you have insurance on the collar?"

She looked taken aback. "Why would you ask?"

"Something that valuable should be insured."

"Yes, we have insurance," her husband said.

"But that doesn't bring back the fact this collar was a reward for Sugar's first blue ribbon. That is something we cannot replace." Mrs. Westford glared at me. "If it wasn't for your dog, this wouldn't have happened."

I raised my brows. "Your cat came here on her own. If it weren't for Caper, you wouldn't be holding at least some of the diamonds." I snuggled my pup under my chin. "You're a good girl," I crooned.

"Isn't there a leash law here?" Davis glanced from one to the other.

"Yes, but the cat ran out when I had the door open talking to Ms. Turley about her dog's horrible behavior." High spots of color appeared on Mrs.

Westford's cheeks. "She's a high-strung animal and doesn't like a leash. The dog wasn't on one earlier."

Which reminded me. How did Caper get out in the first place? Since she seemed to find trouble when let loose, I always left her in the house, on her lead line, or on a leash with me. "May I go, please?"

Davis nodded. "I'll come by your place when I'm finished with the Westfords."

I stepped outside and glanced to house number seven where Eric lived. Seeing his jeep and his side-by-side parked out front, I headed in that direction. He opened the door before I reached the steps.

"Hey, gorgeous."

"Hey, yourself." I tilted my head. "Did you let Caper out earlier? Before you told me about her chasing the cat?"

"No, I saw the two running around, then Mrs. Westford flagged me down. Why?"

"Because I distinctly remember shutting her in my house." I went on to explain the rest of the day's happenings.

"Come on, Hershey. We're checking out CJ's house." He stepped aside so his chocolate lab could join us.

"You really think someone let her out?" It didn't make sense. Why? Usually when someone messed with my dog, it was because I'd poked my nose where it didn't belong.

He shrugged. "Let's go find out." He put an arm around my shoulders. "I was kind of hoping we could get through the Christmas season without a mystery."

"That would've been nice." I leaned into him,

grateful for his warmth. "It's so cold today."

"Yeah, February cold, not December. No campers across the lake, so work is slow. Gives me time to get some things done around the house," he said, walking me home.

"What can you possibly do in a tiny house?"

"I've been watching shows. You know I like to cook, and one episode showed a tiny house with a pantry and spice rack that pulled down from the ceiling. I'm going to build one."

"Wow. That sounds amazing." I wanted one. I already had one in the floor storage where I kept things I didn't use much, but every inch of a tiny house could be utilized if one knew how. Maybe I needed to watch less true crime and watch what Eric watched to get ideas of my own.

"Stay outside." He put a hand on the mace clipped to his belt and pushed my door open. Unlocked. Had I forgotten again?

He glanced back and raised his eyebrows, holding the door open for the dogs to enter first.

My mouth opened and closed. "I got nothing." I really couldn't remember if I'd locked it in my excitement to decorate the tree.

Not hearing any barks or growls, Eric and I stepped inside. Nothing seemed out of place. I was good at putting things away when I'd finished with them. A house this size could clutter very quickly, so I could tell it was exactly as I'd left it. Strange. "Why let the dog out and not take anything?" I glanced around to locate my cat, Sherlock. He sat on the windowsill barely sparing us a glance.

"Are you sure nothing is missing?"

"Pretty sure. I don't keep anything valuable here." After the first rash of thefts, I'd rented a safety deposit box at the bank. Of course, I didn't really have a lot of valuables to begin with. My friend, Ann Lowery, cop turned private detective, rented my grandmother's house. I did have a few mementos there, but nothing someone would want to steal. I plopped on the sofa. "This has something to do with the diamonds." I heaved an exaggerated sigh and slumped. Sherlock leaped onto my lap. "Someone used Caper for their own rotten gain." Again. Why did this keep happening to me? "Sherlock could have escaped and been lost."

"Chin up, sweetheart." Eric sat next to me. "This is mild in comparison to some of our other adventures. Want me to call Anne?"

I rolled my head to face him. "Do you think we need to?" Anne always got roped into being my bodyguard when danger loomed over my head. "The Westfords seem to be the target this time. Someone just used my dog as a distraction." The thought made me feel a little better. No involvement meant no danger to me or my friends. "Want to stay for supper?"

"Sure. What are you fixing?"

"A hearty potato soup for a cold day like this."

A knock sounded at the door. Knowing Eric the way I did, I stayed put and let him answer. Always the gentleman, my man. He opened the door and let Davis in.

"Tell me again your version of the story, and you'll be done." Davis sat in the chair across from us.

I repeated what I'd told him. "That's it. Oh, and

someone let my dog out as a diversion."

"What?" His eyes narrowed.

"I distinctly remember leaving Caper in the house when I went to the center so she wouldn't be under foot. Someone let her out. She chased Sugar. Sugar went home. I went to the Westfords, the cat got out. The cat ran to the center and climbed in the tree. Mrs. Westford retrieved said cat and noticed the collar was missing. We returned Sugar to the house and fetched Caper. You know how she loves diamonds." I smiled. "Then we found the collar with half of the diamonds missing. Voilà. End of story."

"Did the cat have the collar on when she darted out the door?"

"I don't know. She's pretty fluffy. It could have been easily hidden in her fur."

The pieces were clicking in his brain. "How far behind you was Mrs. Westford?"

"She arrived at the building before me."

"Hm." He pushed to his feet. "Okay, let me know if you remember anything else."

"I will."

Eric escorted him out, then leaned against the door. "He's got a suspect in mind already."

"Good. I'm content to sit here." I propped my feet on the coffee table and crossed my ankles, then remembered I was supposed to be fixing supper and let my feet fall to the floor. With two dogs and a big man, moving to the small galley kitchen took some maneuvering. I loved this little house, but if I were ever to get married, I'd have to move back into Grams's house.

I couldn't help but wonder whether Davis

would check the financial records for the tenants of house number fifteen. Not that I would ever have enough money to buy a thousand-dollar cat or a diamond-encrusted collar, but if I did, I wouldn't have anything left after. I glanced over my shoulder. "Do you think the Westfords could have done this for the insurance money?"

Chapter Three

I couldn't help it. I'd lain awake late into the night pondering how to find out whether the Westfords were trying to commit insurance fraud. Getting involved really was an addiction for me, one I had no idea how to break.

Ugh. I climbed out of bed and padded downstairs for a cup of coffee, doing some fancy footwork to keep from tripping over Sherlock who insisted on rubbing against my ankles.

I popped a pod into the coffee maker and stared out the window over the sink. The day looked as cold as yesterday. Frost covered the ground. Winters were slow not only for Eric, but also for myself. As manager of the campground and tiny houses, my main job was to lease the homes, or sell in some cases, and do one or two rides around the campground each day.

Some people might think my life boring, but I loved the simplicity of it. Coffee finished, I added creamer and folded down the two-person table from the wall. I set my laptop on top and booted it up to check for emails.

No new inquiries for rentals. Not a surprise this close to Christmas.

I closed my laptop and headed back upstairs to get dressed. Fifteen minutes later, I clicked a leash on Caper, checked and double checked that my front door was locked, and headed for the campgrounds in my cart with Caper wagging her tail beside me.

Just because there weren't any campers didn't mean there wouldn't be something that needed doing—kids partying, etc. It warranted me checking. Eric helped, but he had a much larger area to patrol.

I took the path past our little glass-walled chapel. The building was my pride and joy since its restoration. The cross that lit up at night could be seen from almost everywhere in the community and campgrounds. Everything looked fine.

Wait a minute… I stopped the cart and looked closer.

The chapel door hung open a couple of inches. I might forget to lock my own front door, and while the chapel was never locked, the door was always closed. I sighed. If people didn't take better care to keep the weather and critters out, I'd have to rethink the open-door policy.

"Come on, Caper." I led the dog inside the chapel and stopped to listen. No running footsteps, no slamming of the door to the storage room. All seemed in order, but I ventured forward anyway.

Footprints appeared halfway down the aisle. They led through the side door and disappeared. Whoever left them had gone into the woods behind the chapel. I called for Caper to follow, then let the footprints lead me.

It didn't take long for me to see the first sparkling, dropped diamond winking at me from the dried fallen leaves. Would the jewels leave a trail like Hansel and Gretel's breadcrumbs? Since I didn't know how far ahead the jewel thief might be, I returned to my golf cart. As I continued the drive to the campgrounds, I called Davis with my phone on speaker. "You know that path behind the chapel?"

"Yes."

"I found a diamond on the ground."

Davis sighed. "Please tell me you aren't getting involved."

"I'm not. I'm doing my job, noticed the door to the chapel was left open, followed the—"

"All right, I get it. I'll meet you at the chapel in twenty." Click.

I'd have to hurry to circle the campground. What I really wanted to do was stay at the chapel and follow the glittering trail. That would only result in more disapproval from Davis, and I'd had enough of that to last me a lifetime. It had been a very busy year.

I sped around the grounds, then circled back to the chapel. The campground was asleep for the winter, and I hadn't spotted any signs of kids goofing around after hours. If I had, then Eric would step in, since enforcing the rules was his job. Breaking them was mine. I grinned and hopped off the cart to greet Davis.

"Come on, I'll show you." Rather than lead him through the chapel, we went around. "See?" I pointed to the gem.

"You only found this one?" He bent and used a cloth from his pocket to pick up the stone.

"Yes, I didn't go any further. I've learned my lesson about venturing out on my own."

"Sure you have." He glanced up the trail. "Let's see if we find any more."

Yay, he was letting me come along. A rare treat, indeed. I mean, I would have followed regardless, but it's nice to be invited.

"Stay behind me and be quiet."

Good ole Davis. Sweet as always. I took the end of Caper's leash to prevent her from running ahead and followed the detective, scouring the ground for anything sparkly.

We found nothing. The dropped diamond wasn't part of a trail.

"Keep your eyes open," Davis said. "The thief might be back."

"For the rest of the diamonds?"

"Maybe. The collar is at the station, but the thief doesn't know that."

"You think the Westfords are committing insurance fraud, don't you?" I arched a brow.

"What makes you think that?"

"A gut feeling."

"Don't ask any questions, CJ." He marched down the path, refusing my offer of a ride, saying walking helped him think.

Very well. I still needed to drive the loop of the community.

Roy Olson, our local handyman, stepped out of his house and waved for me to stop. "Number fifteen is really getting on my nerves."

"What are they doing?"

"They want me to build a see-through cat tunnel that goes up and around the house." He crossed his arms.

"That isn't your job."

"They seem to think I'm their personal servant. I need you to put your foot down. I'm hired to do repairs, that's it."

Yep. It was going to be a long six months. "I'll talk to them." Cat tower. Ridiculous. Plus, the Westfords were renters, not owners. They couldn't do major construction to the house, and I seriously doubted whether the other tenants would want a cat tower if the house wasn't rented.

I secured Caper's leash to the cart and approached the Westfords' front door. I knocked and stepped back, prepared to scoop up Sugar if she tried to escape.

A laughing Mrs. Westford opened the door. "Yeah?" She seemed to have gotten over yesterday quick enough.

"I must inform you that we cannot fulfill your request about the addition." There. That sounded official and authoritative.

"This place really doesn't care about the happiness of its residents." Her smile faded.

"You are renting, Mrs. Westford. That type of construction could prevent us from renting the house to someone else after you've vacated the property."

The woman stared at me, stony-faced, for a moment, then she slammed the door in my face. "Lee, you'd better figure this mess out so we can leave this horrible place," her voice echoed through the door.

Figure out what? How to retrieve their collar? The insurance money? Or something else entirely? I decided to keep a close eye on the occupants of number fifteen.

"What cha doing?" Mags pulled up alongside of me.

"Come back to the house and I'll tell you."

Back home, I made coffee for the two of us and told her about finding the diamond and the silly request of the Westfords. "Want to help me spy on them?"

"Do I? Silly question. Winters bore me to tears. With your Uncle Larry working such long hours at the youth center, he doesn't have a lot of time to spend with me." She blew into her mug. "What do you want to do first?"

"Stakeout?" I wiggled my brows. "It'll be cold, but we can wrap up in blankets."

"Let's do it."

Chapter Four

"This is like old times." Mags snuggled down in a thick quilt. We'd "borrowed" Larry's car since the Westfords wouldn't recognize it.

"Not enough time has passed for old times to fit here." I wrapped my hands around a thermos of hot coffee and stared at number fifteen.

The occupants still moved around inside at ten p.m. Sugar sat in the window. I'd bet she could see us, knew what we were doing. I shuddered. The cat might be beautiful, but her owner gave me the creeps.

"Say what you will." Mags cut me a sideways glance. "I miss having a mystery to solve."

"You're rarely the one almost killed."

"Nonsense. I'm usually right there with you. Except for the flight over the mountain. I'm too old for that."

I chuckled. Only Mags was allowed to mention her age. Not yet sixty, Mags wasn't old, at least I didn't think she was. Eccentric as she was, Mags was my best friend. I preferred older people, really.

Especially after tending to Grams for so many years.

The door to the house opened. I squinted to see better. Mr. Westford closed the door and strode toward the front of the grounds, shoulders slumped against the cold. Who went for a walk this late on a frigid night?

"Come on. Let's follow him, but be quiet." I carefully opened my door.

Mags pretended to lock her lips, not that it would work, given past events. Still, she'd be silent for a few minutes before she couldn't help herself.

Staying low and keeping to the shadows as much as possible, we kept our eyes on Lee. The man stepped outside the gate and glanced both ways up and down the highway.

"He's waiting for someone," Mags whispered.

"Shh." I pulled her behind the dumpster and put a finger to my lips. Thank goodness it wasn't hot weather. The last time we'd hid here, we were surrounded by very unpleasant odors.

Lee pulled a cell phone from his pocket. "Where are you? Kim is going to notice me gone soon. I'd really like to put an end to all this." He listened for a few seconds. "Fine." He whirled and stomped back into the community.

I shrugged at the wide-eyed Mags. Who was on the other end of the conversation, man or woman? I motioned Mags forward and followed Lee back to his house.

His wife immediately started screeching, "Where were you?"

Uh-oh. The man wasn't very good at sneaking around.

"Just walking, dear. I've got a lot on my mind."

"You need to be worried about our investment in that collar." Her shadow through the curtains crossed its arms. "We're broke, Lee."

"I'm well aware of that, dear. That's one reason I've got a lot on my mind. Good night." His shadow headed up the stairs, I presumed.

"I'm not finished talking to you," his wife said.

We weren't learning anything here, other than the fact that things weren't rosy in the Westford household. Feeling bad for eavesdropping on a private, if unhappy moment, I pulled back.

A yeow sent me lunging forward. A white flash darted past me. Sugar had escaped when Mr. Westford either left or returned.

"Now what?" Mags asked.

"We catch the darn cat and return her. I'll say I was doing my last round before going to bed." As manager, it was plausible.

I gave chase, Mags quickly falling behind. Sugar ducked under house number six where the Flower family resided. Lucy would kill me if I woke up her kids.

"Here, kitty, kitty, kitty." *I'm going to wring your neck.*

Sugar hissed and swiped at me. Of course, she wasn't declawed. My hand burned where her nail scratched.

"You like fish? I've got a can of tuna with your name on it."

The cat sprang away from me.

I sighed and crawled from under the house and continued my pursuit, passing Mags who now leaned against the car sipping her coffee. "Thanks for the help," I said, rushing past.

"No problem," she called after me. "I'm here if you need me."

I rolled my eyes and raced after Sugar as she headed for the community building. Now I had her. There was no way she could get inside. My shoulders slumped as she jumped and squeezed through a partially open window. Would I have to lock the building after hours? I'd hoped to provide a place for the teenagers to hang out of the cold.

Pushing open the door, I stepped into the dim room, lit only by the twinkling lights of the Christmas tree. "Here, kitty, kitty, kitty." *Please don't be in the tree again.*

She wasn't. Instead, she happily sharpened her claws on an easy chair in the corner. Destructive little beast.

I closed the window, turned on the overhead light, and unplugged the Christmas tree, already forming the notice I'd hand out tomorrow about how to leave the clubhouse before leaving. After shutting off all means of escape for the feisty feline, I headed to the corner.

"Come on. I've had enough of your shenanigans." As I stooped down to pick her up, my gaze landed on the back of chair where the upholstery had pulled away from the frame. How had I not noticed that before? I seriously doubted a cat could have torn it away.

I peered behind the fabric. Aha. A gift box. One of the fake presents I'd set under the tree as part of the décor. I pulled it out and opened it.

Loose diamonds blinked up at me.

Something hit me in the back of the head. The last thing I saw before blacking out was diamonds scattering across the polished wood floor.

The first thing I saw when I woke was a single diamond staring me in the eye. I put a hand to my head, relieved not to find any blood on my fingers, and inched to my feet before picking up the gem and dropping it into my pocket.

I groaned and stepped outside. Not seeing any sign of the trouble-making cat, I shuffled to where Mags still waited, although she'd moved to the car's interior.

"What happened to you?" She asked as I slid into the driver's seat.

I explained. "Did you see anyone?"

"No, but I closed my eyes for a few minutes." She pressed the button on her watch. "Look at that. It's after eleven. Way past my bedtime."

"I got hit in the head, but I'll call Davis in the morning." I drove home, which took all of two minutes.

"Should I stay with you?" Concern flickered across Mags' face.

"I'll be fine." It barely hurt, although I'd most likely have a dickens of a headache in the morning. "Call me at eight. If I don't answer, call the morgue."

"Not funny, Clarice Josephine." She shoved open her door and got out. "I'm going to call you every half an hour."

"Please don't. I'd really like a good night's sleep. I didn't get a nap like someone I know."

"Don't pout. It causes lines around your lips."

She closed the door and entered her house.

Since I wasn't an idiot, I didn't go straight to bed when I got home. It was hard to resist teasing my friend. Instead, I let Caper out to do her business and leaned against the railing of my postage-stamp porch.

Whoever hit me hadn't targeted me. I was simply in the wrong place when they came to retrieve the diamonds. What bothered me was the fact I hadn't heard them enter the room. There were only two places to hide in the clubhouse. The bathrooms. The kitchen area wasn't closed off.

Had they taken Sugar, or had the cat ran out when my attacker did? I glanced toward number fifteen. I had to know whether the cat made it home safely. Pain in my rear or not, it was my tenants' beloved pet.

I reached into the house, grabbed Caper's leash off a hook, then clipped it to her collar. I wasn't going anywhere without a warning system, and my dog was perfect for the job. A few minutes later, I stood in front of number fifteen and stared at the open door.

Chapter Five

Here we go again. I'd landed smack dab in a mystery I didn't want.

Gravel crunched behind me. I gasped and whirled.

Eric crossed his arms. "Mags called me. Why are you out here after getting knocked on the head?"

"I wanted to make sure the cat made it home. Instead, I see an open door. I was just about to call the police."

Appeased, he pulled me close. "Are you okay?"

"A dull headache. Nothing serious." I leaned against him, called the local police, and was told Milton, one of the officers on duty, would arrive soon. "Should we look inside?"

"No." Eric rested his cheek alongside mine. "We wait."

I understood going inside would contaminate a potential crime scene, but curiosity tugged at me like a laser beam. I stretched, trying to peek over the steps.

Eric chuckled. "Relax, Milton is here."

The officer pulled to a stop in front of the house. He shook his head as he strolled toward us. "CJ Turley, do you ever stop nosing around?"

"Trouble seems to find me." I grinned. "You police officers might get bored without me."

"You do keep us on our toes." He climbed the steps and paused in the open doorway.

I followed and peered around him. The house looked as if the occupants had merely stepped out and forgot to close the door. "Where's the cat?"

Milton glanced over his shoulder. "Outside if the door was left open long enough."

Caper yanked the leash out of my hand and raced to a nearby bush. She set up a frenzy of barking, sure to wake not only the dead but the living as well. "Caper, hush." I grabbed the end of her leash and pulled.

She yelped, then resumed barking harder. I separated the branches of the bush and spotted a very irate Sugar. "Found the cat."

"I'll get her." Eric reached down and smooth-talked the feline until she curled up in his arms and purred.

I glanced at Caper. "She doesn't usually act this aggressive toward another animal. These two must have gotten into a scuffle."

Milton exited the house and pulled the door closed. "Everything looks fine inside. They must have not closed the door properly. Anything else?"

Sighing, I told him about getting hit in the head.

"Lead on." Milton gave an exaggerated bow.

I went with Milton while Eric returned Sugar to

her home. "The diamonds had been stuffed into that chair." I pointed to the one in the corner.

"Did Davis tell you there are teeth marks on the cat's collar? Have you checked your dog's pooh for diamonds?"

"You think Caper stole the collar and ate the diamonds?" I raised my brows. "Then why would someone hide the diamonds? Why hit me?"

"I don't have all the answers. It's just a theory. But that dog of yours has a thing for diamonds." He scoped out the room, then declared it empty.

True. Caper enjoyed sparkling things. "Now what?"

"We keep trying to find out what happened and keep you out of trouble." He flashed a grin and ushered me outside. "I'd make this a crime scene, but it's so contaminated now it would do no good."

"Don't go to any trouble on my account. It's not the first time someone cold-cocked me." I doubted it would be the last considering my penchant for snooping. Maybe I should start wearing a helmet when I leave the house. Since I'd been up long enough not to be concerned about falling asleep, I curled up on the sofa, covered myself with a crocheted blanket, and fell asleep as soon as my head hit the pillow. When I woke, both fur babies lay on top of me, I stretched, then padded my way to coffee. Couldn't start my day without it, especially since I'd had a very long day and only a few hours of sleep.

The Westfords' car sat in front of their house, so I made plans to let them know about the open door. I'd leave the fact that my dog might have been the first thief of the collar to Davis. My tenants didn't seem like fans of mine, so no need to increase their dislike.

Glancing to where Caper waited at the door to be let out, I couldn't help but wonder whether she was guilty of taking the collar off the cat's neck. I grabbed my coat and stepped outside so she could do her business. "A simple imprint of your teeth will tell, won't it?" I gasped.

If she were guilty, I wouldn't have to pay, would I? I couldn't replace one diamond much less half a collar's worth. "Oh, Caper, you've been a naughty girl." I called her back into the house and resumed my wakeup routine.

After showering, getting dressed, and eating toast and jam, I shrugged back into my coat, locked Caper in the house, double-checked the lock, and drove my cart to house number fifteen. Nine a.m. was a decent hour to knock on someone's door, right?

Before I got out of the cart, Danny, Roy Olson's son, ducked around the corner, then dashed across the street. The sixteen-year-old hadn't been in trouble since I took the job, but his behavior bordered on suspicious, like the time he'd stolen my laptop. I gave chase, cornering him against an empty rental.

"Hello, Danny."

"CJ." His features fell.

"What are you up to? I want the truth. I'm too busy for games, and if you're up to no good, I'll tell your father."

"I'm trying to solve the mystery." He scuffed the toe of his shoe in the dirt.

I tilted my head. "How do you know about that?"

"I overheard Mags talking to Larry."

"By listening outside her house?"

He exhaled heavily. "It's Christmas break. I'm bored, so I wander around. I can't help it if folks leave their windows open."

"You wouldn't hear anything if you stayed on the road. Get in." I motioned my head toward the passenger seat.

"Are you going to tell my dad?" He moved as if walking the Green Mile.

"Not this time, but I am taking you home." Summer break was easier on the boy since I'd hired him to mow the grounds here and at the camp. I'd try to find something constructive for him to do during the winter.

I stopped in front of his house, the largest in the community. It wasn't as large as the Flower family's house, but Roy did everything for Heavenly Acres that I couldn't. "Did you hear anything?"

Danny's face lit up. "I sure did. I overheard Mr. Westford telling his wife that everything was going according to plan."

"That isn't much." I frowned.

"She replied that if that nosy manager would mind her own business, things would be smoother."

Aha. That would be me. What kind of plan did they have going?

"Then they started arguing about someone that Mr. Westford keeps sneaking out to see at night. That's when I left. I didn't want to hear anything gross."

"I don't blame you." I smiled and drove back to number fifteen once Danny slid from the cart. I'd used his eyes and ears before to help gather information, but if he were going to do it again, I needed to know at least, so I could watch out for him.

With no more interruptions, I knocked on the door. Mrs. Westford yanked it open. "What now?"

"Good morning," I sang, determined to be cheerful despite her surliness. "I'm here to inform you that your door was left open late last night, and nobody was home. I called the local authorities who came out to investigate. We found Sugar under a bush and put her back into the house." My grin widened. "I thought you would want to know."

"Lee?" She turned around. "You left the door open last night."

"Sorry," he called from the loft.

"Thank you." Mrs. Westford made a move to close the door.

"Is there any news on the diamonds?" I wanted to keep her talking to see whether she'd give me a clue as to whether she was behind my attack.

"No. Besides, it's no concern of yours any longer."

"Actually, it is." I told her of chasing Sugar into the clubhouse and finding a bag of diamonds. "Someone knocked me out and took them. You wouldn't know who, would you?"

"Are you accusing me of something?" Her eyes narrowed. "If Sugar was out, then you would also know we weren't home. Didn't you just tell me my door was left open?"

I shrugged. "Doesn't mean you couldn't have circled back. Have a good day."

That ought to flush her out, if she was

responsible and/or committing insurance fraud. I'd found that antagonizing a suspect seemed to make them careless. The Westfords were the only suspects I had—the only ones the police had, too, unless Davis was withholding information from me. The only time he readily shared was if we were working together.

Maybe it was time to pay a visit to Ann. Since the prior cop was now a private investigator, she had access to information I didn't.

Chapter Six

"Hey, CJ," Anne greeted me with a smile when I rang her doorbell. "I wasn't expecting you."

"I took the off chance you'd be home." I removed my coat and hung it on the antique coat tree by the front door. "I have a favor to ask."

"I've heard of the latest mystery you've gotten involved in."

Ah. I'd forgotten about her boyfriend at the precinct. "I'm wondering if you can find out what Davis knows, and if there's any dirt on the Westfords."

"Sure. Want some tea?" She headed for the kitchen.

Returning to Grams's house always seemed a bit surreal to me. I'd spent five years caring for her as cancer slowly wasted her body away. That's probably why I couldn't live here yet. "That sounds wonderful. Thanks."

Tea in hand, I sat on the familiar tweed sofa and told Anne everything that had transpired over the last couple of days. "Milton suggested Caper took the collar. That would mean the theft after was one of convenience. Which might blow my theory of insurance fraud."

"Not necessarily. Who could have taken advantage easier than the Westfords?" Ann sat across from me.

"I can't think of anyone. Anyway, I've accused her. Now to wait and see what happens."

Anne rolled her eyes. "Deliberately inviting danger."

"How else can I find out?" I wiggled my eyebrows. "I've been lucky so far."

"Luck has a way of running out."

True. "Let me know if you find out anything."

"I'll know something, even if only a little, by tonight. Want me to bring over a pizza?"

"That sounds great." I headed home to do some household chores while I waited. Mags was peeking out her front window, It wouldn't be long before she came over to see where I'd gone. It took two minutes. I wasn't even out of my car.

"Come into the house," I said, stepping out of my car. "I'll make coffee."

"Great. I'll fetch the leftover cake." She rushed back to her house.

By the time she returned, lemon pound cake in hand, I'd already let Caper out to relieve herself and waited on the porch for my friend. "I'm assuming you want to know the latest."

"I have to admit I'm surprised to see you out and about after being attacked." She pressed her lips together and sniffed. "You should have asked me to go with you."

"I only visited Anne." I popped a pod in the coffee maker.

"To have her dig up information?"

I nodded. "On the Westfords." I told her about the teeth marks on the collar. "I'm expecting Davis to take an imprint of Caper's mouth at any moment. I've openly accused Kim Westford of hitting me. The ball is rolling."

"Why not make it roll faster?" She grinned. "Throw a Christmas party at the clubhouse and have those interested draw names. Make sure you get Kim's. Then, make sure the gift you give her has something to do with her faking the theft. That ought to do it."

I laughed. "You have an evil mind, my friend." The idea did hold merit. "What could I give her?"

"A book on insurance fraud. Fiction, of course. If she's guilty, she'll get the picture."

"You should have been in law enforcement." I handed her a mug of coffee and prepared my own.

With one week until Christmas, I'd have to move fast to plan a party. "Could you ask Larry what kind of budget he'd let me have? I need to work on fliers and put them up right away."

"Sure. You know he can't refuse you anything." She carried her coffee to my table for two and sliced the cake. "You were already going to have a party. Why haven't you started planning?"

"I got sidetracked with the whole missing-collar thing." Now, time was running out, and I prided myself on community get-togethers. Once a month was what I aimed for.

A knock sounded on the door. I opened it to see Davis. "Hello."

"I need an imprint of Caper's teeth."

"What took you so long?"

He shook his head. "Milton has a big mouth." He pulled a flat piece of…something soft from his pocket. "I put bacon grease on it to make it more enticing. Here."

I took the whatever it was. "Afraid she'll bite you? Caper doesn't have a mean bone in her body." I knelt and placed the thing in her mouth. She bit down. "Good girl." Poor thing looked offended when I removed it. I handed it back to Davis and fetched my pup a real treat.

"How's the head?" The corner of Davis's mouth twitched. "Knock any sense into you?"

"Ha ha." I wrinkled my nose. "Don't you have work to do?"

"Yep. Mags, Amber and I would like to have you over for supper tonight. You and Larry."

"That sounds wonderful." She smiled over her cup. "I'll bring dessert."

"I'm counting on it." He planted a kiss on her cheek and left.

"To think he wasn't always my favorite person," she said. "Regardless, he can't know of our plan to trap Kim Westford."

"He's more likely to get the tip from you than from me." I resumed my seat at the table and opened my laptop. "Let's do a potluck. As people respond to my invitation, I'll pair them up for the gift exchange."

"Or—" She held up a finger, "Why not do a

week-long thing? A Secret Santa exchange, revealing the final gift at the party. You could really make Kim sweat."

"You're a genius." My fingers flew across the keyboard. Half an hour later, I'd sent out emails to every resident and printed a cute flier to hang on the community board.

"Larry said you had all the money you need within reason." Mags slid her phone into her pocket and pushed to her feet. "Let me know if you need anything else from me. I have to go bake a chocolate cake."

"Doing it potluck style won't cost much. We'll supply paper products and drinks."

"Let's have an ugly Christmas sweater contest, too. Those are always fun."

By the time Anne arrived with the pizza, and Eric showed up, since we usually ate supper together, I had an affirmative response from everyone. Even the Westfords.

"You look pleased with yourself," Eric said, kissing me.

I explained why. "Now I need to find the perfect book for my secret pal."

"Mega meat." Anne set the pizza on the table. "Why wasn't I invited to this party?"

"You don't live here," I said.

"No, but my landlord does." She opened the box and plopped a slice on a plate.

"Why do you want to steal the joy of Christmas by giving a gift to someone that will only upset them?" He held up a hand to stop my protest. "I know she's a suspect, but…it's Christmas."

"If Davis is right about Caper being the original culprit, my dog might have already stolen Christmas. Especially, if I have to pay for the missing diamonds."

"You won't have to. You never had them, they've gone missing, yada yada," Anne said. "You can't fault a dog for chasing a cat."

"Especially *that* cat," I muttered, reaching for a slice of mega meat. "Did you find out anything on the Westfords?"

"They filed for bankruptcy. Lost a big house, a second car…they're involved in cat shows up the Yazoo. They've spent a lot of money on that cat."

"And intended for the diamonds to be their saving grace." I pursed my lips. "Steal them, get the insurance money, and have all that money back. But why not put rhinestones on the cat's collar and keep the money? No one would know the difference."

Anne shrugged. "People are weird."

Sherlock growled from the windowsill. His tail flicked back and forth like a pendulum.

Eric parted the curtains. "Sugar is out again."

"I ought to let Sherlock out so he can father some mixed-breed kittens. Wouldn't that rile Kim Westford?" I grinned. "I'm getting tired of chasing down that cat for people who can't take proper care to lock her inside."

"That's the pot calling the kettle," Eric said, smiling.

"Hey, I lock Caper up now. Someone else let her out this time." And I still hadn't found out who or why, other than to create a diversion. "If she was let out for the sole purpose of stealing the collar, then someone knows of her love of diamonds. This was all planned."

"Wasn't it mentioned in the newspaper during the diamond thefts?" Ann's brow furrowed. "Someone is following your infamous career in troublemaking."

"This must be 'pick-on-CJ' day." I bit into the pizza. A pepperoni slid off onto my chest. Great. A greasy stain on my favorite sweatshirt. I sighed and scrubbed at it with a napkin. I refused to let their jokes upset me. I'd solved worse crimes and lived to talk about them. This time would be no different.

Chapter Seven

The sound of my front window shattering jolted me awake. Caper darted downstairs, her barks ringing in my ears.

No shuffling for me that morning. Having something crash through a person's window woke them up faster than two cups of coffee. I dashed down the stairs after Caper and scooped her up before she could run across the broken glass.

A rock with a sheet of paper wrapped around it lay in the middle of the room. A blast of cold air came through the broken window.

"Hush, Caper." I closed her in the bathroom, then called Eric before heading back upstairs to get dressed in something warmer than my pajamas. By the time I came back down, my man stood in the living room, staring at the rock.

"If you get me a broom, I'll sweep this up." He bent and picked up the rock, unwrapping it. "*Stay out of it*," he read. "Maybe they don't know you after all." The corner of his mouth twitched.

"Ha ha." I handed him the broom. "Funny how this comes right after our conversation last night. Maybe someone stood outside the window and listened to us. It could have been Lee or Kim coming for Sugar."

"Makes sense. Someone must have heard us talking to know you were involved. Call Davis."

After I made the call and swept up the glass, Eric and I headed outside to search for clues. The lack of rain had left the ground hard as cement. No footprints appeared under the window.

I stepped back to the road's edge and raised my hand as if to throw something. "I think they were about here." Where would they have run to? I'd rushed down the stairs. They couldn't be far.

Hands on my hips, I surveyed the area while Eric studied the ground. "Eric?" I took off after a man in a dark hoodie. "Hey!"

He glanced back. I didn't recognize him. His eyes widened, and he took off at a run toward the front entrance.

Eric passed me with little effort. I was fast, but nowhere near as speedy as my six-foot-two boyfriend. As he caught up with the fleeing suspect, Davis pulled up.

"That was fast." I bent over, trying to catch my breath.

"I was close by." He marched to where Eric held onto a struggling teenager. "What's going on?"

"These freaks started chasing me," the boy said.

"Why'd you run?" Eric released him.

"When two strangers yell and come after you,

you run." The boy straightened his hoodie.

"Why are you here?" I straightened.

"I spent the night with Danny Olson. Cheez." He glared.

Davis narrowed his eyes. "Know anything about a rock through this woman's window?"

The boy paled. "No."

"Did you see anyone outside besides you?"

"Sure. I saw a man jogging. He wore black sweatpants and a gray hoodie."

"What's your name?" Davis pulled a small notepad from his pocket.

"Ryan Johnson."

"Tell me everything you can about this man."

"That's it. He was jogging. I didn't think anything wrong about it. Look, I got a job, and I'm going to be late."

"Hold on." I glanced around the area, instinct telling me the boy lied. "How do you plan on getting to town? I don't see a car."

The boy whirled and sprinted for the road. Davis and Eric gave chase, leaving me to wait behind. I'd had enough exercise for the day, thank you, and it wasn't eight o'clock yet.

A couple of minutes later, Ryan was brought back by Eric and Davis, handcuffed, then put into the backseat of Davis's car. "The jogger paid him twenty dollars to throw the rock," Davis said. "He'd never seen the guy before. He stopped Ryan when he left the Olson house."

"The jogger could be anyone." Although I couldn't picture Lee Westford jogging. "If you got close enough to take money, you saw his face," I said through the car window.

"It was just a guy." Ryan hung his head.

"We'll question him some more," Davis said. "I suggest you board up your window and let me handle this. Things are escalating."

I nodded and stepped closer to Eric. "Want me to make pancakes?"

"Is that your way of bribing me to take care of the window?" He grinned.

"Yep."

"I'd do it for nothing." He put an arm around my shoulders, leading me home after Davis pulled away with Ryan in the back of his car.

"I know you would, but I doubt you've eaten."

"Nope. I threw on some clothes and came the instant you called me." He turned me to face him. "I'll always come to your rescue."

A slow smile spread across my face. "I know you will."

His kiss drove away the morning's cold, warming me from the inside out. When we pulled apart, I leaned my forehead against his chest. I could stay there forever if not for the plaintive grumbling of my stomach.

We strolled hand-in-hand back to my place. I glanced at number fifteen. "Remember when house number ten was where all the action happened?" That lot still sat empty. "Obviously, it wasn't the house. It's time to put a new tiny house on that spot."

"Silly girl. It's always the people." Eric grinned.

I nodded, but after so many bad people living on that lot, I'd had the house removed. I wasn't superstitious, not really, but that house had seemed to be cursed. "Now, I need to get inside number fifteen and see whether Lee owns a pair of dark sweatpants and a grey sweatshirt. See if he has running shoes."

"I still can't see him jogging anywhere."

"Neither can I." The pudgy man looked as if the most exercise he got was from the sofa to the fridge. "But I want to make sure." Somehow, I needed a really good excuse for entering the house. As manager, I could at any time if I gave the resident a day's notice. Maybe it was time for an inspection.

Chapter Eight

In order to make things "fair," I sent fliers to every resident who rented about a cursory checkup in two days. No one cared. It was in their contract after all.

Bad thing was, my idea increased my workload. Good thing was, I got to see everyone's Christmas decorations, which I loved. Not that they could go full-out in such small spaces, but every bit of Christmas cheer brightened my spirits. Until I reached house number fifteen.

Mrs. Westford waited on the front porch, Sugar in her arms. "Make it quick." She stepped back from the door.

Darn. I'd hoped she wouldn't be home. Hard to snoop with her looking over my shoulder. "I will." I flashed a smile, hoping it looked genuine, and stepped into the house. They'd sure managed to fill it with clutter since moving in. I thought Mags' place was crowded with knickknacks, but this house with all its porcelain cats had hers beat.

"How do you keep Sugar from knocking over your things?"

"She is very sure-footed."

I headed for the bedroom at the back. Number fifteen was one of the few houses without a bedroom loft. "Does Mr. Westford enjoy jogging?"

"You're joking, right?"

I faced her and shrugged. "We're thinking of starting a jogging club. Just curious."

"The man goes to work, comes home, kicks off his shoes, and sits on the couch until bedtime. Then, after I'm supposedly asleep, he sneaks out to meet his mistress. Foolish woman." She laughed at my expression and sat on the sofa. "Of course, I know about her. I'm not blind."

I opened my mouth, then snapped it closed. Their marriage woes were none of my business. I riffled through the clothes in the closet, dug through the hamper, and didn't find any sign of sweats or running shoes. I couldn't spend too much time snooping, or Mrs. Westford might get up and come see what I was doing.

"Thank you. I look forward to seeing you at the party." I brushed past her, having second thoughts about whether the Westfords stole their own diamonds or not.

It was apparent neither of them jogged. I needed to find out whether Davis had gotten a description out of Ryan. It wasn't fair that the detective expected me to divulge every tidbit of information I dug up, but he could withhold from me. Law enforcement or not, he should share.

I was also having second thoughts about gifting

Kim Westford a book on insurance fraud. Christmas was a time of kindness. I'd find another way to bait the Westfords. I rubbed my hands together. Time to go shopping. After picking up Mags, I headed to town. "I'm excited now."

"You're a strange one, CJ." Mags shook her head. "But I'm not one to turn down shopping in a gift shop."

Neither was I when it was for someone else. I didn't like clutter in my own home, but this shop carried porcelain cats.

I picked up a kitten ornament, an adult coloring book picturing cats, and a sleek twelve-inch sculpture. That would be the final reveal. I also couldn't resist two dog ornaments, one that looked like Caper and one that resembled Hershey. Cute and whimsical.

Mags bought enough animal miniatures to fill Noah's ark. "These are for me. I need to find fine teas for Tammy Olson. I drew her name for the exchange."

"Want to go to the coffee shop? My treat." I rarely turned down the opportunity for a frozen mocha. "Maybe you can find a special teacup for Tammy."

"Sounds good. We can sip our drinks and discuss the next step in Operation Fraud."

Mags bought several flavored herbal teas, then joined me with her coffee at a round table. "That man keeps looking at you."

I turned in my chair. "Which one?" The place was crowded.

"Blue jacket with his back to you," she

whispered. "He keeps glancing over his shoulder."

My phone buzzed, distracting me from the man whose face I couldn't see. I glanced down to read a text from Ann saying she had the jogger's description. Mid-thirties, white, dark hair, medium build, brown eyes. I sighed. That fit a lot of people. It also fit the man who apparently kept watching me.

I glanced up and met his dark-eyed gaze. When I narrowed my eyes, he turned back to the cup in his hands.

"So, how are we going to draw out the thief?" Mags tilted her head.

"Shh," I whispered. The man who'd been glancing at her stiffened and sat back in his chair at Mags' question. "I don't think this is the place to talk."

"People talk business around here all the time. No one cares what others are conversing about."

"He does." I stood. "Come on." I headed for the door and directed Mags around the corner of the building. I peeked around the corner to see the man exit the building and glance both ways. He was looking for us.

I withdrew and plastered my back against the block wall. When the man strolled by us, I grinned. "Hello."

His eyes widened and he increased his pace.

"Did you have something to say to me?"

He kept walking.

"I don't think he likes the fact you figured out what he'd been doing," I said.

"Then he should have been more subtle." Mags hitched her shopping bag on her shoulder. "Let's get our treasures home. We can talk there."

We picked up sub sandwiches for lunch and went to my house. "How are you going to hand out your gifts?" Mags asked. "I haven't decided. I can't very well walk up and hand them to Tammy."

"Why not ask Rose Flower to take it and not reveal who sent the gift?"

"Good idea. Tammy might think Lucy is the Secret Santa. It will totally throw her off."

"I'm going to set mine on Kim's porch each night before going to bed." That way, I could also get a good look around the grounds. If I was lucky, I might spot our jogger up to no good.

"Have you heard anything from Amber about who Davis thinks is guilty?" I bit into my Italian meat sub.

"She won't tell me anything other than his original suspect doesn't look like a suspect anymore. Whatever that means."

I frowned. "That means he no longer thinks the Westfords are guilty."

"That puts us back at square one."

"Yeah." I set my sandwich down. All Lee was guilty of was seeing his mistress, a woman his wife knew about. Caper might have pulled the collar off the cat, but someone else knew the diamonds were real. How? Did the Westfords go around talking about how much the collar was worth?

"The cat show." I snapped my fingers. "That has to be where the outsider discovered the collar's worth." I searched the web for the next cat show. Tomorrow. "Want to see some fancy cats? I guarantee the Westfords will be there. It isn't too far of a stretch to expect the thief to be there, too."

"Sure. It might be fun." Mags grinned. "We should bring our cats and show those fancy felines what a real cat is."

I laughed. "Sherlock would not be pleased. He hates the carrier." I bore some scars to prove it. "From the photos, it looks fancy. People dress up."

"Like cats?" Mags' brows rose.

"No. In nice clothes." I rolled my eyes. My friend would wear something bright and monochromatic. Mark my words.

Mags stood and tossed her sandwich wrapper in the trash. "I'll be ready in the morning. Don't do any investigating without me."

"There isn't anything to do until the cat show. I'm going to study cats so I don't sound like a complete idiot tomorrow."

"Good luck." She laughed and went home, leaving me shaking my head at her not-so-funny attempt at humor.

After cleaning up from lunch, I curled up on the sofa with my fur babies and my laptop to learn what I needed to pretend I knew something about cats other than that they purred and landed on their feet. The show the next day had the list of entries. Sugar Westford would be participating.

Good. Hopefully, I'd catch sight of someone overly interested in the Westfords' loss of the collar. Wouldn't the thief be interested in knowing how much information the police had? Wouldn't he want to know if there were any suspects?

I propped my feet on the coffee table and started researching. Yep, something would pass hands at the show, and I intended to be there when it happened.

Chapter Nine

The next morning, I dressed in wide-legged slacks, black flats, and a sparkling sweater. Since I'd never gone to an animal show, I had no idea whether I was overdressed or under.

After making sure Caper's and Sherlock's stomachs were full, I stepped outside. Mags strolled across the street in a bright fuchsia sweater dress with matching gym shoes. Around her shoulders was what I hoped was a faux mink shawl. I laughed. "Glad you didn't disappoint in your attire."

She preened. "I know how to dress for the occasion, young lady."

I stifled another laugh and climbed into the driver's seat. I'd already texted Eric where we were going, knowing he'd receive the message when he got to where he had service. Sometimes getting service on the mountain was impossible.

"Did I tell you when I went to leave my Secret Santa gift for Kim, Lee was leaving? Again."

"I'd never stand for that behavior from my

man."

"Neither would I."

"On a more pleasant note, I'm very excited," Mags said, petting her shawl. "Once I'm familiar with these shows, I may enter Callie. She's a purebred calico, you know."

"Maybe you could enter her into the Moggie category." I snorted. Mags' spitting cat was definitely not moggie material.

"What's that? The cat version of a muggle? You know, non-cat as opposed to non-magical? Non-magical people are called muggles…" I waved my hand in dismissal as I realized she had no idea what I was talking about.

"It's where the cat is judged on temperament." I grinned.

"Oh, she would win that for sure."

"Really? Callie makes Sugar look like a meek kitten. You do not have a nice-tempered cat."

"I suppose Sherlock would do better." She crossed her arms.

"I'm pretty sure he's a mutt, but he does have a nice personality." I pulled into the parking garage after an hour of Mags' cold-shoulder treatment. "Keep your eyes and ears open. I guarantee you the thief is here."

"I know what I'm doing." With a swish of her shawl, she exited the car and marched toward the entrance.

Running to catch up with her, I apologized. "Callie is a very fine cat."

"Hmmph."

"You no longer agree?" I bit my lip to keep

from smiling.

"I'm done with this conversation. Let's catch a diamond thief." With great dramatics, she flung the double doors open, struck a pose, then strolled in as if she walked the red carpet at the Oscars. Crazy dress or not, I now felt very dowdy.

Heads turned, some stared, others looked as if they should know who Mags was, then shrugged when they couldn't place her. My friend should have been on the stage, the way she loved the spotlight. "Where do we start?" She whispered. "I can only act as if I know what I'm doing for so long."

"Let's find the Westfords." I paused in front of a tabby so still when its owner dangled a feather in front of it that I thought the cat was stuffed.

"Prince is very obedient," the woman said. "He always earns high marks."

"He's gorgeous." I smiled and continued to where a flat-faced, white cat hissed and swatted at everyone that walked past. Definitely not moggie material there.

We passed cats of all colors and breeds, in all stages of readiness for their moment in the judge's eye. We found the Westfords in the back of the building. Sugar sported a pink bow on her head and a new collar around her neck. I doubted the sparkling gems were real this time.

"I could have used you last night, Lee," Mrs. Westford glared at her husband and ran a brush through Sugar's hair. "You knew today was important, and not only to me and Sugar. I thought you wanted to recoup our losses with another big win."

"I do, but I feel claustrophobic in that tiny house." He studied the nails on his right hand. "I told you I have everything under control."

"Is it the house or me that makes you claustrophobic?" She clamped her lips tight when she noticed us.

"We came to wish you luck," I said, "but if this is a bad time—"

"No, it's fine." Kim resumed her brushing. "Sugar needs calming, though. Give her a pat and move on. I don't mean to be rude, but I need to focus."

I raised my brows and glanced at Mags, then patted the top of Sugar's bow. The cat ignored me like her owner and licked her paw. "Good luck." I forced a smile and stepped away.

"No matter how nice you try to be to her, she's rude." Mags sniffed and pulled her shawl off her shoulders.

"She's having a difficult time with the stolen diamonds and a cheating husband." I sent up a prayer for mercy for the woman. I might be testy too if I was going through what she was.

I stopped in an out-of-the-way corner and studied the crowd for anyone seeming overly interested in the Westfords. I spotted the man from the coffee shop almost immediately. He stood behind a table on which sat the biggest cat I'd ever seen.

"That's a Maine Coon," Mags said. "My next cat."

"That won't fit in your house." But it was gorgeous. "It looks as if our eavesdropper is here legitimately."

"Doesn't mean he didn't steal the collar. Let's see how he acts when he recognizes us." Mags strode toward him.

The man's eyes widened, but since he couldn't very well leave his cat unattended, he couldn't run.

"What a marvelous creature." Mags scratched behind the cat's ears.

"Thanks." His gaze flicked to me. "You showing or looking? Cats for sale are in the other building."

"Just looking, not buying." I smiled. "Our neighbors are showing, and we're here for support."

"Right." Mags winked at me. "They've been through some trials lately." She leaned closer to the man. "Thievery and infidelity."

I didn't think it possible for his eyes to widen further, but they did, going almost googly-eyed. "We shouldn't gossip, but are you acquainted with the Westfords?"

"No." He answered rather quickly. "Only seen them at these type of functions."

"Thank you for watching Frederick." A woman in her sixties squeezed up to the stand.

"The cat isn't yours?" I arched a brow at the man.

He gave a quick shake of his head and melted into the crowd. Recognizing suspicious behavior, and going with my gut instinct, I went after him. "Hey."

Shooting me a glance over his shoulder, he ducked into the men's room. Drat. Making sure no one was watching, I followed him in, leaving Mags to guard the door.

"Seriously, woman?" He paled.

"Why are you so interested in me and the Westfords?" I crossed my arms and looked as stern as my miniature frame would allow.

"I'm not."

"Sure you are. At the coffee shop, you were very interested in the conversation I had with my friend. Now, you're here and you don't have a cat."

"Neither do you." He tilted his head.

"Are you the jogger who paid a boy to throw a rock through my window? Did you steal the collar that belonged to the Westfords' cat? Who are you?" I narrowed my eyes.

"Stay out of it. This doesn't concern you." He growled and shoved past me, knocking me to the floor.

My head hit the tiled wall behind me. I didn't even want to know what germs I might be sitting in. When Mags didn't come to my rescue, I used the strength of my legs to press my back against the wall and push to my feet. No way was I going to touch the floor with my bare hands.

After making sure I wasn't bleeding, I washed my hands and turned as a man entered. He jerked back and peered at the Men's sign on the door. "You're in the right place," I said. "I'm the one who is lost." I flashed a grin and stepped out.

Where was Mags? My heart skipped a beat. That man hadn't taken her, had he?

I dug my phone from my pocket.

"Can't talk. Chasing Mr. Jogging Man through the showroom." Click.

Where was the showroom? I thought we were

in it. I asked someone wearing an official-looking vest.

"This is the prep room. The showroom is through those doors." She pointed across the vast room. "You're only allowed in the bleacher section, not the floor. The show starts in half an hour."

I nodded and rushed after my friend. She should never have taken off after the guy on her own. He had to be at least twenty years younger and a lot stronger. What if he turned on her?

I stepped into a room devoid of people. Either there weren't a lot of spectators at a cat show or folks waited until the last minute to pick their seats. I stood and listened, straining to hear past the silence for any sign of Mags.

There. The pounding of running feet.

I headed on a sprint in that direction, catching a glimpse of Mags, dress hiked around her knees, racing across the red show ring. I guess no one told her that area was off limits. Making sure no staff was around, I took off after her. "Mags."

She stopped, breathing hard. "Thank the good Lord. I'm winded. You go." She pointed with one hand and handed me her Taser with the other.

I grabbed the Taser and ran.

Jogging Man barged through a set of heavy back doors. "Stop. I only want to ask you some questions."

He flipped me an obscene gesture and slammed the door behind him. Rude.

I went through the doors a little more carefully then he had. My head still ached a little from meeting the men's-room wall. I didn't want another concussion. Why did bad people think hitting me over the head was the way to go?

As I stepped outside, Jogging Man, now on the back of a motorcycle, sped past narrowly missing me. He had to be the one responsible for hiring Ryan. Whether he'd actually stolen the diamonds or knew the Westfords was left to be discovered.

I entered the main room. Cats and their owners took up position behind podiums. A quick scan of the small crowd in the bleachers located Mags easy enough, thanks to her bright-colored dress. I made my way to her, careful to stay on the outskirts of the show ring. "What were you thinking?" I shook my head. "He knocked me to the floor in the bathroom. He could have done the same or worse to you."

"You let him get away, didn't you?"

"He sped off on a motorcycle. I couldn't exactly keep up."

"Do you think he knows the Westfords?"

I shrugged. "No idea, but I'm pretty sure he paid Ryan to throw the rock. What I don't know is why, unless he's involved, which he must be." My shoulders slumped. We were getting nowhere fast.

She snapped her fingers. "I have an idea. At the party, we'll talk about what happened today close enough to the Westfords so they can hear."

"Yes." I smiled. "They'll think we know more than we do. If one of them is behind all this, it might draw them out. I'd really like this solved before Christmas."

"That would be nice. We don't want a cloud hanging over a special day." With a satisfied smile, she focused on the happenings below us. "Oh, good.

Sugar got a blue ribbon. That should make Kim Westford happy enough to answer any questions you might want to ask. Are you delivering another gift tonight?"

"Yes, the last one before the party, but I go late so she doesn't see me. Questions will have to wait." I was pretty sure her good nature would carry over until the next evening. I no longer thought her capable of stealing the diamonds. My money was on her husband. Caring for a wife and a mistress had to be expensive.

All I had to do now was prove it.

Chapter Ten

The evening of the community Christmas party, I donned a red sweater with a felt reindeer head covering the front. Right in the center of my chest was a blinking red bulb to serve as the reindeer's nose. I might not win for the ugliest sweater, but I doubted this sweater would ever see the light of day again.

Eric picked me up in a sweater the color of pea soup with dogs wearing Santa hats running across the front of his chest. "I put the last of the supplies in the clubhouse. Ready?" His eyes widened as I turned on Rudolph's nose. "The men are going to be staring at your chest all night."

"What little I have, you mean." I wiggled my eyebrows and linked my arm in his. "Let's go catch a thief."

He grinned. "That has become your favorite sentence lately."

"Better than let's go catch a killer. This is much safer."

Our laughter carried us across the road and to the community center. The party would start soon, but I had time to make sure any last-minute details were in order.

Mags and my uncle, Larry, arrived first, followed by Amber and Davis. They weren't members of the community, didn't expect to participate in the gift exchange, but did bring food. Davis figured I was up to something and wanted to be there to get me out of any trouble I might find.

"It's a party, Davis." I rolled my eyes and took the potato casserole from his hands. "Try to enjoy yourself, and don't look like a cop, please." He'd scare away the thief.

Soon, the laughter and excitement of the community's children filled the room, drowning out the adults' conversations. I eyed the stack of presents under the tree, grateful for Larry's donation for gifts for the children since they weren't part of the Secret Santa exchange.

The Westfords arrived last and sat at a table. Davis watched them with narrowed eyes, as did I. From their body posture, they weren't pleased with each other. I prayed a fight wouldn't break out and ruin the party atmosphere.

Soon all the tables filled with people and plates piled high with food. No one seemed to be acting suspicious at all. Maybe Jogging Man was the sole person responsible for the theft. I shrugged. The Christmas party would have taken place either way. I took my seat next to Eric and decided to enjoy myself and let what would come…come.

"People aren't doing anything but eating."

Mags stabbed a meatball with her fork.

"Maybe we were wrong about the Westfords." I glanced up to see Davis's reaction to my comment.

He kept his focus on his plate, but a muscle ticked in his jaw. Interesting.

"Do you have a prime suspect yet, Davis?"

"Why do you insist on calling me by my last name? You know my name is Bill." He scowled.

"Habit." I grinned. "Well?"

"Yes, I have a suspect, and no, I'm not going to tell you anything more." He resumed eating.

"Maybe I won't tell you what I know." I dug into my pasta salad.

His plastic fork slapped against his paper plate with a dull thwack. "Since you've mentioned it, you'd be breaking the law by not saying anything."

"The two of you are more entertaining than a movie," Eric said, laughing. "But you might want to keep your voices low. You're attracting attention."

"CJ makes me lose all reason." Davis shook his head. "What do you know?"

I lowered my voice and leaned forward to tell him about Jogging Man. "I wasn't able to get his name."

"You were attacked and didn't tell me?" High spots of color appeared on Eric's cheeks.

"No, I simply fell when he pushed past me."

"What's the difference? You were injured."

"Barely."

"Save it for later," Davis interrupted. "You said this guy followed you to the coffee shop?"

"Did he?" I glanced at Mags.

"He came in after we did," she said, "and took

a seat at the closest table. But we didn't know he would be at the cat show."

"Could he have followed you there?"

"Possibly," I said. "We were busy looking for the Westfords. You know, to wish them luck."

"Right." Davis smirked and rose to his feet, then carried his empty plate to the trash bin.

"You really do antagonize him," Amber said, smiling. "If you could only hear his frustrations when you get involved in another crime."

"I can imagine." I sensed the children growing restless. "Time for gifts."

With Eric acting as Santa, all gifts were handed out. Turned out Tammy Olson had my name and gifted me with a wonderful oil painting of Caper in a dark wood frame. "I love it. I didn't know you could paint?"

She smiled. "I don't have as much time as I used to but try when I can."

"I'll treasure it. Thank you." I knew just the spot to hang the painting. It would fit perfectly between the two windows above the sofa.

I smiled as Kim Westford carried the cat sculpture to me. "This is lovely. Thank you."

"It reminded me of Sugar, in a sleek rather than fluffy way. There's also a plug in the bottom to use it as a secret hiding place. Maybe for when you get the collar and diamonds back."

"Don't tell Lee, but I've already received the collar back." She turned and headed back to her table, setting the sculpture in the center and fiddling with it for a moment, before returning to the front of the room where those participating in the sweater contest gathered. Her sweater with a cross-stitched resemblance of Sugar wasn't ugly in the slightest. At least not when put against Mags' pooh-brown sweater with elves and twinkling lights. My friend won the contest hands down and received the prize of a gift card.

"To buy a new sweater," Eric said, handing her the card.

"What's wrong with my sweater?" Mags arched a brow. "It wins every ugly sweater contest I've entered. I think I'll keep it."

An angry shout rose above the frivolity.

Conversations ceased as everyone turned to Kim.

Hands on her ample hips, she glared around the crowd. "Where is my present? Where's Lee?"

I whirled to face Davis. "Was Lee around when you returned the collar?"

"Yes. I gave it to them outside before the party started."

"Kim must have put it in the bottom of the cat and Lee saw her. He's the thief."

Davis darted outside, me on his heels, Eric and the others right on mine. Of course, Eric caught up and passed me on our race toward house number fifteen.

The shattered pieces of the sculpture lay on the front porch. One missed diamond sparkled from the wreckage.

"Stay here." Davis reached for the doorknob, halting as a car sped from the back of the house.

"He's gone." The taillights disappeared through the front gate. "You couldn't have known

Lee was the thief," I told Davis. "Or you wouldn't have given them the collar."

"No, I thought it was Mike Royson. You know him as Jogging Man."

I narrowed my eyes. "How did you figure that one out?"

"Because he's a known thief, and a certain somebody described him as one who might have stolen a woman's ring." He groaned and marched back toward the clubhouse. "You should have come to me with your suspicions."

"I wasn't sure yet."

"Did you catch the rat?" Kim waited for us in front of the building.

"No, ma'am." Davis planted himself in front of her. "Do you know where he might have gone?"

"To his girlfriend's house, most likely."

"Do you have her address?"

"Of course, I do." She gave an evil grin. "Lee thinks he's sneaky, but I've known all along where he goes at night. I've got it written down at home. Her name is Ginger Smith. A stripper name, if you ask me."

We trooped back to her house. She muttered a curse when she saw the broken sculpture. "Lee had better not have let Sugar out."

"I'll get you another sculpture," I said, relieved to see her cat watching us from the kitchen counter when Kim opened the door.

Lee had definitely left in a rush. Several of his wife's figurines lay shattered on the floor. On purpose, maybe? Through the open bedroom door, I could see scattered clothes.

"I'm going to kill him." Kim opened a kitchen drawer and pulled out a flowered address book. From a slit in the fabric that covered the book, she pulled out a slip of paper and handed it to Davis. "Keep it. I have it memorized."

Davis handed her a business card. "Call me if your husband shows up or you see him anywhere around."

"I'll be standing over his corpse when I call."

"Ma'am, that is not funny."

"I'm not joking."

The two stared at each other for several long seconds. Davis was the first to break away. Outside, he ordered us not to follow him into town.

Fine. I returned to Kim. "Could you write that address down for me? If I find him before the detective does, I'll let you know."

"Promise?"

"I promise." While I'd let Davis know when Kim went to confront her husband, I didn't want the man dead, so I'd let her know right before I called the police.

She scribbled the address on a piece of paper. "It's a trailer park on the other side of town. Be careful. It's seedy." She handed me the paper and closed the door.

"You aren't going tonight, are you?" Eric asked.

I shook my head. "I've seen that side of town. It's scary enough in the daytime."

"That's my girl." He bent down and kissed me before walking me home. "Take Mags and her Taser with you when you go. Good night, sweetheart. See you tomorrow."

I let Caper out and leaned against the railing of my porch, hoping she'd hurry up with her business. The night had turned bitter cold, biting through my sweater. My painting. I'd left it on the table at the clubhouse. "Come on, girl. I need to lock the place up."

The trashcan overflowed inside the clubhouse. Some tables still held dirty dishes and wrapping paper. It might be past ten p.m., but I couldn't go home, leaving the place that messy. I bagged the garbage, pulled another trash bag from under the small kitchenette counter, and then cleared the tables, leaving the painting where it was. I'd fetch it after taking the garbage to the dumpster.

Caper moved around the room eating dropped bits of food until I took the broom from the closet and started sweeping. Hating the broom, she hopped up on a chair and curled up to stare at me with soulful eyes.

"Sorry, sweetie." I hummed Christmas carols as I worked, mulling over in my head what had transpired.

Lee Westford had stolen his own diamonds, hid the fact from his wife, hired someone to intimidate me, all because he had another woman in his life? I shrugged. Immorality caused people to do awful things. I'd seen it before. Too many times. It saddened me.

I did what I could to bring justice to the world, and while I'd suspected Lee, I hadn't figured out the whole thing. Now, the diamonds were gone again. I seriously doubted he or his girlfriend would still be around by morning.

Leaving Caper where she lay, I put the broom away, hefted one of the bags of garbage over my shoulder like Santa Claus, and headed for the dumpster. It took several swings before I pushed the heavy lid up and over. Then I headed back for bag number two.

Caper opened one eye, then closed it again. "You'll have to come home with me when I'm done, silly pup."

I grabbed the last bag and returned to the dumpster. It weighed less than the first one and only took one hefty swing. There. I could sleep well, knowing I didn't have the mess to deal with in the morning. I could have asked Roy to take care of it, but the man had enough work to do.

Turning, I froze at the figure of a man standing in the shadows. With a cry, I turned to run. He caught up with me and yanked me around to face him. His hands circled around my throat. Lee under the hoodie.

Shrill barking meant rescue was on its way.

Caper bit down on Lee's leg, shaking with her entire body. He released me and tried pulling her off. He aimed a punch at her head. She let go and he kicked her away. Cursing, he dashed back into the night, leaving me short of breath and grateful for my furry little protector.

I scooped her into my arms and sprinted for home, smart enough to know he'd come for me again when the opportunity presented itself. I couldn't be caught outside.

Chapter Eleven

"What happened?" Mags peered at my neck.

"I had a run-in with Lee last night. Caper saved me." I tied a scarf around my neck to hide the bruises. "We need to stop and speak with Davis before heading to the trailer park."

"Do you think Lee will be there?"

I shook my head. "I'm hoping his girlfriend, Ginger, will be there and feeling talkative."

"Did you tell Eric?"

"He was asleep when I arrived home, and now he's up in the mountain somewhere. I'll tell him later." He wouldn't take the news lightly. My man took it personal when I got in trouble as if it were his fault he wasn't there. It couldn't be easy being my boyfriend.

The receptionist at the police station informed us that Davis was out and wouldn't return for a few hours. That left us with no other course of action but to pay a visit to Ginger.

I drove to the address Kim had given us and studied the white mobile home with pink trim. Flowerpots, devoid of blooms because of the winter season, hung along a wooden porch erected to make the trailer look more like a house. Ginger might be a homewrecker, but she appeared to have some pride in where she lived.

"I don't see any sign of Lee, do you?" Mags leaned forward and stared. "I've got my Taser, though…just in case."

"Good girl." I didn't see any sign of the man or his car. "Let's see what we can find out."

I approached the house slowly, my gaze darting in each direction for signs of danger. It wouldn't surprise me to see Lee jump out from the evergreen bushes on each side of the porch. I touched the scarf at my neck, last night's events fresh in my mind. I wouldn't mind a little payback when I came face-to-face with Lee again.

"There's murder in your eyes," Mags said. "You might want to get rid of that look if you don't want to scare the woman away."

Good point. I pasted on a smile I hoped wasn't a grimace and approached the front door.

A red-haired woman opened the door before I could knock. She looked about forty, with maybe an extra twenty pounds on her frame— not exactly pretty but pleasant-looking enough. "If you're selling anything, I'm not buying," she said, taking a sip of coffee.

"No, ma'am. We're here to ask whether you've seen Lee Westford."

"Why are you asking? I already told the cops I

haven't seen him in two days." A flicker of worry crossed her features. "He's in trouble, isn't he?"

I nodded. "He's guilty of insurance fraud and trying to kill me." I pulled the scarf away from my neck enough for her to see the bruises.

Her eyes widened. "He's gone off the deep end. Come in." She stepped back so we could enter. "Too many nosy neighbors."

I sent up a prayer that Lee wasn't waiting for us inside, then entered a cozy home smelling of vanilla from a nearby burning candle. A small tabletop Christmas tree added some holiday cheer. I felt as if Ginger and I could've been friends if we'd met under different circumstances.

Ginger motioned for us to have a seat on her floral sofa. "You must think me a horrible person, spending time with Lee when he's married."

"We aren't here to judge," I said.

Mags snorted and rolled her eyes. "I'll try to be charitable in acknowledging that Kim can be a difficult woman. Did you know what he was up to?"

"No." Ginger sat across from us. "Lee loves me—he really does. If I didn't know how much before, I do now. I've been diagnosed with cancer and need surgery I can't afford. Lee told me not to worry about a thing. He had it all taken care of." Tears welled in her eyes. "I had no idea he'd resort to this in order to help me."

Drat. Now, I kind of felt sorry for the man. "The Westfords are financially broke. Or at least they were until Lee decided to steal the diamonds. I never did understand why they didn't sell them a long time ago."

"His wife refused. The cat's collar was a status symbol, I guess. A mask to wear to look prosperous." She wiped her eyes with the sleeve of her robe. "It's all for nothing. He'll go to jail, and I'll die."

Mags reached across and patted her knee. "Chin up. There's always a way."

"Do you have any idea where Lee might be?" I asked. While my heart broke for her, I couldn't let sympathy get in the way of justice. My sore throat reminded me of that fact.

"I have no idea." She broke into sobs. "He's been spiraling the last week, muttering things I didn't understand. Now, it's all clear to me." She fought for control and struggled to her feet. "You're right. I'll proceed with the surgery and worry about the cost later. I'll sell this place if I have to."

"Why don't you?" I stood and took her hand. "I've an empty house in Heavenly Acres that you can live in rent-free until you're back on your feet." Number ten had sat vacant for too long. My uncle wouldn't mind once he knew the circumstances. "Think about it."

"I will. Thank you."

"Will you be safe here alone with Lee clearly out of his mind?" Mags asked.

"He would never hurt me. I do think you should keep a close eye on his wife though. He really dislikes her and in his mental state—"

True. We needed to have protection assigned for Kim. I handed Ginger a business card. "Please, call me or the police if you see Lee."

She nodded. "Detective Davis came by last night. He also gave me a card, but I didn't spend much time talking to him. He searched the house and left. I hope you find Lee, I really do, and I hope he survives this ordeal. I'd rather have him in prison than dead."

As for me? I was torn between the two. An attempt on my life would do that. I thanked her and reminded her again about the house I had for her if she were interested, then headed back to the police station.

Davis must have pulled into the lot seconds before we did because he was marching up to the double doors when we pulled in. I tapped the horn. He turned and came to us.

"Find out anything?" He asked.

"Good morning to you, too." I grinned. "No, we haven't found out anything."

"Lee tried to kill CJ last night," Mags blurted out.

Davis paled. "I'd say that's worthy news."

I showed him my bruises. "Caper saved the day. Did you know Ginger has cancer and Lee promised to take care of her medical bills?"

He exhaled heavily. "You went to visit her?"

"Just left there. She said he's been different the last week or so. A lot on his mind."

"I'd say so. It can't be easy trying to steal from yourself, hide the fact from your wife, care for an ailing mistress, all while trying to act like the victim." Davis crossed his arms. "It would take a toll on any man. I'm glad you aren't dead, CJ, but you might not be as lucky next time."

"We think you should have an officer guard Mrs. Westford."

He nodded. "I'll have a squad car drive by on a regular basis. Go home and stay there. This case will be over soon, and Eric will kill me if something happens to you."

When he entered the building, Mags and I headed back toward home. "I'd hoped to find out more," I said, "but we did find out why Lee is doing this."

"Doesn't stop the fact he's gone bat crazy and needs to be behind bars."

"No, it doesn't." I glanced in the rearview mirror. "Don't look now, but speaking of the devil."

She turned in her seat. "He's coming up on us fast. Do you think he saw us at Ginger's?"

"I'd bet on it." I pressed the gas pedal. As I sped up, so did Lee.

"He's going to run us off the road."

"Most likely." I made sure my seatbelt was firmly in place. "I'm not a race car driver."

"You're barely a driver at all. Go faster."

"The faster we go, the harder we'll crash."

"So, you want him to catch us?"

"Not really." I increased our speed and tightened my grip on the steering wheel. Don't let us die, Lord, please.

My head snapped forward as Lee rammed us from behind.

Mags dropped her Taser and fumbled on the floor for it.

I whipped the wheel and spun the car around, speeding across the median and back toward the police station. Lee followed, cutting off a semi. The truck jackknifed and flipped. The man was definitely insane. Innocent people were going to get hurt before he finished his rampage.

"Got it." Mags held up her Taser just as Lee pulled alongside us and sideswiped us.

Horns blared. Cars careened out of the way. My small sedan was no match for his larger, older model.

"We can't beat him." My heart beat in my throat. "Call Davis."

Mags looked torn, then finally set her Taser on the dashboard and called her son-in-law. "We found Lee. That's the good news. The bad news is he's trying to run us off the road. He's already crashed a semi. We just passed mile marker 108." She nodded. "You'd better be faster than fifteen minutes. We might not make it that long." She hung up. "He's coming."

I swerved to avoid a slower car in front of me and ended up mired in the ditch. "We'll have to make a run for it." I shoved open my door as Lee skid to a stop beside us.

"Get in." He pointed a gun at my chest. "Both of you."

Something banged on the trunk of his car.

"Do you have Kim in there?"

"Sure do. Let's go. Now."

Mags and I scrambled into the backseat. "Where are we going?" I asked.

"Somewhere no will find three annoying women. Use those zip ties to tie each other's hands together. Don't try anything funny or I'll kill you slow and easy."

I did Mags' hands, then held mine out for her to secure mine. The longer we cooperated, the longer we would live. I fell back against the seat when Lee slammed his foot on the accelerator.

"Please tell me you have the Taser," I whispered to Mags.

"I did but dropped it again. It's under his seat."

"Shut up or I'll shoot you both right here."

We shut up.

Chapter Twelve

I stretched my foot, trying to dig the Taser out from under the front seat. Lee jerked the car to the right, slamming me against Mags and pressing her against the door. A yelp came from the trunk. Kim wasn't faring any better than we were. Still, the car would stop at some point and we outnumbered Lee three-to-one. No man in his right mind would go against three angry women.

We bounced down a dirt road and across a creek. I knew where we were headed. Lee was right. If he killed us at the quarry, our bodies would be easily buried.

He hit the brakes, sending us crashing against the back seat. I bent and fumbled for the Taser, wrapping my fingers around the handle, then sliding the weapon into my pants. It wouldn't be easy to retrieve, but it was the best thing we had.

I smiled knowing Davis would be able to track our phones. All we had to do was stay alive long enough for him to find us. Which he would. He had yet to let me down.

After Lee had me and Mags get out of the car, he opened the trunk and hauled Kim out. Not an easy task because of her size.

She stumbled to her feet, spitting mad. "I'm going to kill you, you worthless excuse for a man."

"Don't antagonize him," Mags hissed.

Kim whirled to face us. "Don't tell me what to do with my own husband."

"Maybe I should let the three of you kill each other." Lee laughed. "Stand on the edge of that giant hole in the ground." He motioned with the gun.

I stood and stared down, fairly certain I could survive the fall. If I jumped, how far could I get before a bullet struck me in the back? "You don't have to do this, Lee. You can't help Ginger if you're behind bars."

"What do you know about anything?"

"I know you want to help her with her surgery. That makes you a man with a good heart."

"He's as crazy as a rabid dog," Kim spit. "Where's Sugar?"

"Wandering around Heavenly Acres." He grinned. "Maybe she'll wander out to the highway. Play a little frogger with the traffic."

Kim lunged at him, her fingers curled into claws.

Lee fired the gun at her feet.

That was all the distraction I needed. I leaped forward and wrapped my arms around his neck, taking him into the hole with me. I twisted my body to put him on the bottom, softening the impact of landing in the packed dirt.

We both lay there gasping like stranded fish. I sucked in air and grappled for the gun as Mags and Kim scrambled down to join us.

Kim took the gun and aimed it at Lee. "I told you this would happen if I found out you stole the diamonds."

"Don't do this." I climbed to my feet, every inch of my body aching. "He isn't worth you going to jail."

"He's ruined us." Tears streamed down her round face. "I resigned myself to the fact he didn't love me anymore. We didn't even buy Christmas gifts for each other; that's how broke we are. I never thought he'd steal the only future we had left."

"It wouldn't have been so obvious if that dumb dog hadn't chased your stupid cat and pulled the collar off." Lee pushed to his feet. "I had the dickens of a time finding the collar and barely had time to remove half the diamonds before people started searching."

"Does this remind you of an episode of *Scooby Doo*?" Mags cocked her head. "'I'd have gotten away with it if not for those pesky kids'? Except this time, it's a little dog."

I bent and sawed the zip tie from my hands on a sharp rock, Mags copied. I reached into my pants and pulled out the Taser.

Mags seemed shocked to see where I'd hidden it. "You can keep it now."

I rolled my eyes. "Kim, use this instead. I guarantee it will bring you satisfaction."

"Not as much as seeing him dead. He's ruined our lives and Christmas."

"Stop being so dramatic," Mags said. "Christmas is still coming. Think of the bright side. You won't have to spend it with him. Let's tie him up, shove him in the trunk, and go home. It's cold out here."

I agreed and stepped forward to threaten Lee with the Taser if he didn't cooperate. Two squad cars roared to a stop behind Lee's car.

Davis, Milton, and Eric sprinted toward us. Davis coaxed the gun from Kim, while Eric took possession of the Taser. "You did good, ladies," Davis said. "I'll take it from here. Mr. Westford. You're under arrest. You should have stopped with the diamonds. Trying to kill CJ means you'll go to jail for a very long time."

"You tried to kill this little snip of a girl?" Kim's face darkened. She doubled up her fist and landed an impressive right hook against her husband's jaw. "I want a divorce."

Eric gently untied my scarf and took a long look at my bruises. After kissing each one, he leaned his forehead against mine. "Will you marry me?"

"What?" My mouth fell open.

"Will you marry me?"

"So you can keep me out of trouble?" My lips twitched.

He laughed. "Darlin' I'm not a miracle worker."

I threw my arms around his neck. "You bet I'll marry you. Whose house will we live in?"

"Well, Anne is in your Grams's house, so I guess we'll put our two together." He pulled me into a hug. "I don't care. I'd live in a tent with you."

Mags clapped her hands. "It's about time. Look, Davis, Eric proposed."

Davis shook his head, pushing Lee ahead of him. "Strange time for a proposal."

"I've got to do it before something really happens to CJ." Eric took my hand. "Mrs. Westford, we'd appreciate a ride back to Heavenly Acres."

"I'm only going back there to find my cat." She stormed past us. "But you're welcome to the ride."

"I'll need you three ladies to come to the station and fill out a report," Davis said, putting Lee in the backseat of his car. "Mrs. Westford, don't leave until that's completed."

~

Christmas morning dawned bright and cold. Eric arrived as the sun came up and woke me with kisses. "Merry Christmas."

I stretched and smiled. "Merry Christmas."

He knelt beside the bed and opened a little black box. "Let's make our engagement official." Inside sparkled a diamond ring. "How does a New Year's wedding sound? I don't want a long engagement."

"That sounds wonderful. The sooner the better. I want to get married in the chapel."

"Of course. There's nowhere else more perfect than that little building you fixed up." He pulled me to my feet. "Let's stay in today, just the two of us and the animals. After the last couple of weeks, I'm yearning for a day of peace."

I smiled and cupped his face. "That sounds marvelous." I couldn't think of a better day than snuggling on the sofa with my man and watching

Christmas movies while the lights twinkled on my tiny Christmas tree.

The End

Check out the next book, Caper Finds a Treasure, by scanning this code.

Website at www.cynthiahickey.com

Multi-published and Amazon and ECPA Best-Selling author Cynthia Hickey has sold close to a million copies of her works since 2013. She has taught a Continuing Education class at the 2015 American Christian Fiction Writers conference, several small ACFW chapters and RWA chapters, and small writer retreats. She and her husband run the small press, Winged Publications, which includes some of the CBA's best well-known authors. She lives in Arizona and Arkansas, becoming a snowbird, with her husband and one dog. She has ten grandchildren who keep her busy and tell everyone they know that "Nana is a writer".

Connect with me on FaceBook
Twitter
Bookbub
Sign up for my newsletter and receive a free short story
www.cynthiahickey.com

Follow me on Amazon

Enjoy other books by Cynthia Hickey

Brothers Steele
Sharp as Steele

Carved in Steele
Forged in Steele
Brothers Steele (All three in one)

The Brothers of Copper Pass
Wyatt's Warrant
Dirk's Defense
Stetson's Secret
Houston's Hope
Dallas's Dare

Fantasy
Fate of the Faes
Shayna
Deema
Kasdeya

Time Travel
The Portal

Tiny House Mysteries
No Small Caper
Caper Goes Missing
Caper Finds a Clue
Caper's Dark Adventure
A Strange Game for Caper

Wife for Hire – Private Investigators
Saving Sarah
Lesson for Lacey
Mission for Meghan

Long Way for Lainie
Aimed at Amy
Wife for Hire (all five in one)

A Hollywood Murder
Killer Pose, book 1
Killer Snapshot, book 2
Shoot to Kill, book 3
Kodak Kill Shot, book 4
To Snap a Killer
Hollywood Murder Mysteries

Shady Acres Mysteries
Beware the Orchids, book 1
Path to Nowhere
Poison Foliage
Poinsettia Madness
Deadly Greenhouse Gases
Vine Entrapment

CLEAN BUT GRITTY Romantic Suspense

Highland Springs

Murder Live
Say Bye to Mommy
To Breathe Again
Highland Springs Murders (all 3 in one)

Colors of Evil Series

Shades of Crimson

Coral Shadows

The Pretty Must Die Series

Ripped in Red, book 1
Pierced in Pink, book 2
Wounded in White, book 3
Worthy, The Complete Story

Lisa Paxton Mystery Series

Eenie Meenie Miny Mo
Jack Be Nimble
Hickory Dickory Dock

A Heart of Valor
The Game
Suspicious Minds
After the Storm
Local Betrayal

Overcoming Evil series
Mistaken Assassin
Captured Innocence
Mountain of Fear
Exposure at Sea
A Secret to Die for
Collision Course
Romantic Suspense of 5 books in 1

INSPIRATIONAL

Nosy Neighbor Series
Anything For A Mystery, Book 1
A Killer Plot, Book 2
Skin Care Can Be Murder, Book 3
Death By Baking, Book 4
Jogging Is Bad For Your Health, Book 5
Poison Bubbles, Book 6
A Good Party Can Kill You, Book 7 (Final)
Nosy Neighbor collection

Christmas with Stormi Nelson

The Summer Meadows Series
Fudge-Laced Felonies, Book 1
Candy-Coated Secrets, Book 2
Chocolate-Covered Crime, Book 3
Maui Macadamia Madness, Book 4
All four novels in one collection

The River Valley Mystery Series
Deadly Neighbors, Book 1
Advance Notice, Book 2
The Librarian's Last Chapter, Book 3
All three novels in one collection

Historical cozy
Hazel's Quest

Historical Romances
Runaway Sue
Taming the Sheriff
Sweet Apple Blossom
A Doctor's Agreement
A Lady Maid's Honor
A Touch of Sugar
Love Over Par
Heart of the Emerald
A Sketch of Gold
Her Lonely Heart

Finding Love the Harvey Girl Way
Cooking With Love
Guiding With Love
Serving With Love
Warring With Love
All 4 in 1

A Wild Horse Pass Novel
They Call Her Mrs. Sheriff, book 1 (A Western Romance)

Finding Love in Disaster
The Rancher's Dilemma
The Teacher's Rescue
The Soldier's Redemption

Woman of courage Series

A Love For Delicious

Ruth's Redemption
Charity's Gold Rush
Mountain Redemption
Woman of Courage series (all four books)

Short Story Westerns
Desert Rose
Desert Lilly
Desert Belle
Desert Daisy
Flowers of the Desert 4 in 1

Contemporary

Romance in Paradise
Maui Magic
Sunset Kisses
Deep Sea Love
3 in 1

Finding a Way Home
Service of Love
Hillbilly Cinderella
Unraveling Love
I'd Rather Kiss My Horse

Christmas
Dear Jillian
Romancing the Fabulous Cooper Brothers
Handcarved Christmas
The Payback Bride
Curtain Calls and Christmas Wishes

Christmas Gold
A Christmas Stamp
Snowflake Kisses
Merry's Secret Santa
A Christmas Deception

The Red Hat's Club (Contemporary novellas)

Finally
Suddenly
Surprisingly
The Red Hat's Club 3 – in 1

Short Story

One Hour (A short story thriller)
Whisper Sweet Nothings (a Valentine short romance)